BOB & BARRY'S LUNAR ADVENTURES

CURSE of the WEREFLEAS

SIMON BARTRAM

templar publishing
www.templarco.co.uk

A TEMPLAR BOOK

First published in 2015 by Templar Publishing,
an imprint of The Templar company Limited,
Deepdene Lodge, Deepdene Avenue,
Dorking, Surrey, RH5 4AT, UK©
www.templarco.co.uk

copyright © 2015 by Simon Bartram

1 3 5 7 9 10 8 6 4 2

ISBN 978-1-78370-075-2
Designed by Winnie Malcolm
Edited by Libby Hamilton and Katie Haworth

Printed in the United Kingdom

IDENTITY CARD

Name: **Bob**

Occupation: **Man on the Moon**

Licence to drive: **space rocket**

Planet of residence: **Earth**

Alien activity: **unaware**

W.A.A.

WORLDWIDE ASTRONAUTS' ASSOCIATION

Chapter one

For the fourth morning in a row, when Bob, the Man on the Moon, woke up, he wasn't tucked up in the cosy bed where he'd fallen asleep. Instead, he found himself curled tightly in a ball in what seemed like some kind of tiny house. Gingerly, he wriggled out through its small door and quickly realised that the tiny house was actually his dog Barry's kennel. He would have been surprised had he not woken on the three previous mornings in the bath, the airing cupboard and the potting shed. The unusual was becoming quite usual.

Barry himself wasn't anywhere to be seen. In fact, Bob's best-ever friend had been missing for three days. He had disappeared, without warning, around the time Bob's sleepwalking had begun. Bob was convinced that there was a link between the two. However, he wasn't sure whether the sleepwalking had somehow scared Barry away, or whether the sleepwalking had actually been caused by the worry of Barry's disappearance. Either way, Bob was upset. Why would Barry leave him?

Bob missed his best-ever friend so much. All around the house there were reminders of him – his rubber bone, his basket, his ball, his bobble balaclava. And curiously too, the smell of dog was becoming stronger, not weaker. Even Bob's pyjamas seemed to stink of pooch. Stranger still, considering Bob had completely lost his appetite, they were also caked in gravy stains, barbecue sauce and meaty grease. The kitchen too was littered with the bony remains of chicken drumsticks, spare ribs, T-bone steaks and lamb

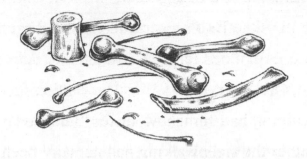

chops. It was a mystery indeed.

Just looking at the mess made Bob feel itchy and no amount of scratching could soothe him. In truth though, it was probably the pesky space dust that was irritating him. Ever since the big scary, hairy asteroid had collided with the Moon, he hadn't been able to scrub it off, not even with his Spacedust Superloofah. (£9.99)

Bob had noticed the asteroid whilst vacuuming the lunar landscape four days earlier. He'd watched, open-mouthed, as it zoomed in from deep space at a blistering pace, its long, red mane trailing elegantly behind it. But there had been nothing elegant about what happened next. Realising it was on a collision course with the Moon, Bob and Barry had leapt, headlong, for the safety of crater 1973. Seconds later... BOOOOOOOOOMMM!!!!!!! The big, scary, hairy asteroid had hit the Moon and bounced back out into the darkness of space. For more than an hour, the universe had shook.

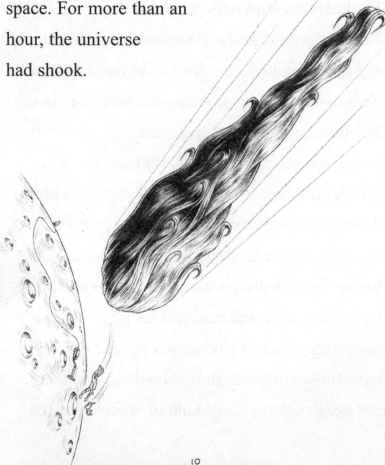

When Bob and Barry had finally re-emerged it was onto a lunar surface shrouded in a pea-souper fog of space-dust, the like of which Bob had never seen before. Worse, until the lunar mist cleared, he would have no idea how much damage had been done to his beloved Moon. For hours the dust had swirled and whirled and crept into any nook and cranny it could find. Even Bob's Moon suit, boots and helmet were no protection. He'd begun to itch immediately and hadn't stopped since.

Bob had been back home for days now, and he was becoming convinced that somehow the asteroid was to blame for triggering the mysterious events – the sleepwalking, the messy house, Barry's disappearance – not to mention the constant itching and scratching.

After yet another vigorous flannel rubdown he still couldn't shift the pesky dust. It was obviously not the usual kind of space-dust. It was thicker and coarser, as if it had some kind of mysterious ingredient to it. It was time, thought Bob, to do some serious investigating.

Chapter two

Bob's dusty old SUPER-DUPER
SUPERSCIENCE KIT wasn't actually that super-
duper anymore. Having finally dug it out from
the cupboard under the stairs, he discovered that
the safety goggles were cracked and the mini-
thermometer was completely missing. Luckily
though, the all-important mini-microscope was
still present and correct.

Carefully, Bob scraped a tiny smidgen of the
dreaded dust from his moon boot and deposited
it onto a petri dish. Then, with one eye squinting,
he closely examined the magnified sample. He
couldn't believe what he saw! The contents of
the petri dish was moving. In fact it seemed to

be ALIVE! The tiniest of tiny creatures were buzzing amongst the particles of dust!

"FLEAS!!!" shouted Bob out loud. "THE SCARY, HAIRY ASTEROID HAS GIVEN ME MOON FLEAS! THAT'S WHY I'VE BEEN SCRATCHING SO MUCH!"

Of course, having Barry as his best-ever friend, Bob was quite familiar with pesky fleas. After Barry's weekly bath (which Barry had whether he wanted it or not) Bob gave him a liberal dusting of Flea-Buster 3000 (£6.99) to repel those itchy little fellows. These ones were different though. They seemed somehow wilder and grumpier and, if Bob wasn't mistaken, surprisingly HAIRY!

Concentrating intently, he studied the miniscule beasties and, with a freshly sharpened 2B pencil, made detailed sketches in his pocket notebook.

Then, after a quick tidy-up of the kitchen, he cycled to the Lunar Hill launch-pad before blasting spaceward to find Steinbeck Trimble's Mobile Library Rocket, scheduled to stop for the afternoon on the backside of Uranus.

Steinbeck Trimble's Mobile Library Rocket was famous for storing every book in the entire

universe. Sadly, none of them could shed any light on exactly what the little critters were and, most disappointingly, not even one of the 5627 illustrations in *The Bumper Book of Midges, Fleas, Gnats and Nits* matched up to the creepy crawly sketches that he had made. Bob was as bamboozled as ever. Then, however, he had a brilliant slice of luck! As Bob placed *The Bumper Book* back on its shelf, an old dog-eared piece of paper fell out from the dust sleeve. Bob picked it up, stared at it and was quite astounded. Skilfully rendered upon the yellowing page was an intricate pen-and-ink drawing of a familiar-looking creature.

If you have encountered such a wee beastie it is of the utmost importance you contact Mr Humphrey Dumpling of 51 Tightrope Lane. The fate of the Earth, Moon and stars could depend on it!

"HOLY HELMETS!!" cried Bob "IT'S A FLEA AND IT PERFECTLY MATCHES THE FLEA PORTRAITS I SKETCHED!"

Bob felt a chill shimmer through his bones. How could simple fleas possibly endanger the Earth, Moon and stars?

The plot was thickening with every passing hour. Bob's brain buzzed with thoughts of hairy asteroids, mysterious notes and everything in between. And, when his brain wasn't buzzing his heart was aching – aching for his dog, Barry. Without his best-ever friend, Bob didn't know how he would put right this topsy-turvy shambles. Staring back at the yellowing page, Bob wondered to himself. Perhaps this Humphrey Dumpling chap could help. Certainly, Bob had nothing to lose.

Back on Earth, he soon found himself knocking on the large, bottle-green front door of 51 Tightrope Lane. An old, roundish man answered and confirmed that he was indeed

Humphrey Dumpling. In turn, Bob introduced himself and showed his notebook. The colour drained from Humphrey's ruddy face and he sighed as if the weight of the universe had been placed on his shoulders. "I feared that one day you would come."

Chapter three

Humphrey Dumpling's home was a feast for
the senses. Squawking parrots and ticking
clocks accompanied the crackling tunes of the
Puddlewick Colliery Brass Band spinning on
a creaky old gramophone. As he was led down
the long burgundy hallway, Bob passed rooms,
left and right, adorned with strange paintings
and artefacts from distant lands. Through half-
opened doors he glimpsed a grand old library,
a greenhouse and a mini-laboratory in which
mysterious experiments bubbled and clinked.
And wafting into every last corner of the house
were the delicious smells of roasting beef and
baking bread.

Humphrey, however, had no interest in giving Bob a guided tour of his home. He was clearly leading him somewhere in particular and, as he walked, he talked.

"Many years ago," he began softly, "I was the owner of the Greatest Flea Circus on Earth and, one day, my global search for new talent led me to the flea-infested beard of Chief M-Parpo M-Pumpo of the last tribes of Inner M-Pooto. His wonderfleas were like no others I'd ever seen and, after much persuasion, the chief agreed to trade me two of them in exchange for my dinosaur-patterned umbrella. I was delighted. His fleas were all singing and dancing superstars, but they came with a grave warning.

"Come full Moon," said chief M-Parpo, "The fleas Hubert and Margot must always, but ALWAYS, be tethered and locked away from the living world for the entire night!"

"At first I heeded his words, but soon the

wonderfleas were making me so rich and so famous that I became blinded by greed. I refused to let even a single night pass without hosting another blockbuster show… not even on the night of the full Moon! And that's when they attacked. After the show Hubert and Margot became more and more boisterous. Soon they began to bully the other fleas. As I stepped in they launched themselves at me and proceeded to bite me on each ear. The cut and thrust of an all night battle followed and it wasn't until the sun replaced the Moon that they tired and I was able to recapture them using my flea-lasso and micro-net.

"A few days later, after much thought, I strapped them into the prop rocket

I used in my show, filled it with ten times the amount of gunpowder it normally required and then blasted Hubert and Margot up into space. I hoped that I would NEVER see them again."

At this point, Humphrey took a breath. It had been some story so far but Bob was still confused. "What was so terrible about a couple of flea bites?" he asked.

A dark shadow seemed to creep across Humphrey's face. "These were not a couple of ordinary flea bites," he answered. "You see, Hubert

and Margot were WEREFLEAS! And Werefleas
are CURSED!!"

"C… C… CURSED?" stuttered Bob.

"Indeed," replied Humphrey. "Whoever they
choose to bite is doomed… doomed to transform
into A WEREWOLF!!!"

"A what – where – what?" asked Bob.

"A werewolf," repeated Humphrey. "A wolf-
man… or woman. A person who, on the night of a
full Moon, transforms into a wolf!!"

As they walked through the kitchen and out
into the garden Humphrey cautiously lifted his
eyes to the pale Moon, just visible in the dusk.

"Tonight will be such a night," he continued,
"and I, myself… am a werewolf!"

And then, with those words, something
INCREDIBLE happened. Suddenly, in front of
Bob's very eyes, Humphrey Dumpling's ears grew
long and pointed and a huge moustache sprouted
out from under his nose. Bob was astonished. For

a few seconds he silently studied Humphrey until, at last, he spoke.

"You don't look much like a wolf man," Bob said sheepishly. "More like a tall elf really… with a moustache."

Humphrey nodded. "That's because I was only bitten twice. My condition is mild – I can control my transformation. But when the Moon has fully risen, yours will be a very different story."
Bobs heart missed a beat. "*My* story?" he cried.

"I'm afraid so," said Humphrey. "Ever since I blasted Hubert and Margot space-wards, there have been rumours of hairy, flea-infested planets, moons and asteroids. That got me thinking. Perhaps the troublesome duo, instead of fading quietly into the cosmos, multiplied over and over and over. Perhaps with every new flea the curse grew more powerful. And perhaps, some way, somehow, they have worked out a way to infect the universe itself, turning each planet, moon and asteroid they meet into something hairy and scary. Your story, itches and sketches have confirmed my worst fears. I believe that the hairy asteroid you encountered was cursed. Within the dust cloud it created, I'm sorry to say, there were possibly MILLIONS of Werefleas. You, Bob, provided them with a hearty lunch, which means you are a complete and utter, one hundred per cent, bona fide WEREWOLF!"

Chapter four

Fortunately, due to his distinguished background in the Puddlelane Amateur Dramatic Society, Bob was a pretty super actor. Now, although he nodded and stroked his chin thoughtfully, inside he was crying with laughter.

What a hoot! Bob was well travelled throughout the universe and never once had he encountered a so-called werewolf. And, even if they did exist, he would be the last person to catch such a condition. He just wasn't the hairy type and he certainly had never wanted to be wild. He was perfectly happy wearing sensible trousers and being polite to policemen and that was that.

By now Humphrey had led Bob to the small potting shed at the bottom of the garden.

"Let's have a nice cup of tea in here," he said. "I do my best thinking in the shed."

Bob was delighted. He never needed to be persuaded to have a nice cuppa and so, happily, he stepped inside.

SSSLLLAAAAAAAAMMMM!!!

In a twinkling the door was flung shut behind him, leaving Bob alone in the darkness. Then he heard the key turn, a bolt rattle and a padlock click. He was a prisoner.

"I'm so sorry!" shouted Humphrey. "But it's for the good of everyone and everything. I'll release you when the full Moon has passed. I PROMISE!"

Then agitated footsteps could be heard leading back to the house.

Bob was stunned. He couldn't spend the night in a stranger's cold and damp shed. He had

important work to do.

Carefully, he searched in vain for a light. As he did so, he stumbled and tumbled over plant pots and crates and spiked his bottom on an upturned pitchfork. Then, from nowhere, an electric pang of anger bolted through his body.

"LET ME OUT OF HERE NOW YOU SNIVELLING LITTLE TOAD," he bellowed, "OR I'LL CREATE A WHOLE DOG-GONE UNIVERSE FULL OF TROUBLE FOR YOU AND ALL HUMANKIND!!"

Bob was shocked to the core. He didn't know
he had such a ferocious outburst in him. "Wow!"
he murmured. "Where did that come from?"
Usually, Bob wouldn't say boo to a goose, but
something inside him was changing. Suddenly
another surge of fury shot through him. This time
he howled like a caged animal.

"I WILL NOT TELL YOU AGAIN!!
LET ME
OOOOOOOOOOUUUUUUTTT!!!"

Again, Bob was astounded. He could feel
his happy-go-lucky self being invaded by some
kind of bad-mannered ruffian. All of a sudden
he just wanted to scream and shout. But, no
matter how much he yelled, Humphrey was
never going to release him.

As the minutes passed, Bob's bouts of anger
became more frequent and more powerful. He knew
he had to calm down. He took deep breaths. He
thought about happy things such as fancy teapots

and chocolate covered nuts. Nothing worked.
The raging force inside was just too strong. Bob
could feel himself slip, slip, slipping away. He just
couldn't hold on. And then, high above the Earth,
the dark clouds parted to reveal the fullest of full
moons above the garden shed of 51 Tightrope Lane.
A bright shaft of moonlight flooded through the
tiny shed's window and lit up Bob as if he were a
rock star on stage. It was then that Bob's eyes came
to rest on a shard of broken mirror and the most
shocking sight he had ever seen.

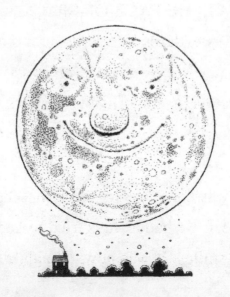

Chapter five

Bob, the Man on the Moon, had never been a hip dude. He liked to be scrubbed up and buttoned down and tucked in and combed through. He was, after all THE FACE OF SPACE and he couldn't let standards slip for even a moment, so it came as a shock to see himself covered in dust and cobwebs, his sensible trousers torn and his astonishingly polished shoes scuffed beyond hope.

But it was his poisonous face that disturbed him the most. He had always tried to keep it bright and smiley. It was now, though, a snarling, growling, portrait of grumpiness. There was no trace of THE FACE OF SPACE. Inside and out, Bob was disappearing, as if some kind of beastly bully was forcing him away, deep, deep down into the depths of nowhere.

However, before he was completely banished, Bob held on just long enough to witness the most frightening part of the remarkable transformation.

It began when his chin sprouted a covering of scruffy stubble, the like of which he had never worn for fear of what the neighbours would think. In seconds the stubble had grown to become a short beard and then grew further to become a long beard. And, as well as growing downwards, it grew upwards, creeping over Bob's whole face, engulfing his eyebrows and forehead before mingling on in with his quiff, which took on a wild new life of its own.

Beneath his tank top and trousers he could feel an animal-like coat of fur sprouting and

watched as it shot out from under his
collar and cuffs.

Next, his fingernails grew
long and sharp, and his toenails
sliced through his ruined shoes. His
eyes became glassy and menacing.
His ears grew large and pointed.
And, in his snarling mouth, most
dramatically of all, he grew huge,
razor-like fangs that dripped with

drool and glinted
under the moonbeams.

The real Bob, helper of little
old grannies across
roads, was
gone. Now,

what was reflected in the
shard of broken mirror was
a smelly, flea-bitten, snot-
snivelling, bona fide one

hundred per cent WEREWOLF!!!

For a moment, the world was so quiet you could have heard a pin drop. Then, to mark his arrival, the Were-Bob rudely broke the silence by cocking one leg in the air, grimacing the most ugly of grimaces and letting off a most almighty, shuddering, shaking FFAAAAAAAAAAAAARRRTT!!! that shook the potting shed and the world beyond. It was a hummer that made even the Were-Bob's eyes water.

The Were-Bob's sense of smell was suddenly incredibly acute. In fact, all of his senses were a hundred times sharper. He had twenty-twenty vision. He could taste the cockroaches without eating them. Beneath his sensitive feet he could feel the woodworm wriggling around in the floorboards. And he could hear clouds drifting across the sky and the sea kissing the shore more than ten miles away.

Most clearly of all though, he could hear Humphrey Dumpling muttering worriedly amongst the bubbling and clinking of his laboratory. Although he was only approximately ten per cent werewolf, Humphrey too had top-class ears. Having heard the shouting, growing and farting, it was obvious to him that Bob was no longer Bob.

"You in th-there," warned Humphrey nervously. "You c-can't leave until the f-f-full Moon has p-p-passed! I'll let you out in the m-morning and I'll m-make e-eggy soldiers. But only if you're g-good!"

But the Big Bad Were-Bob had no intention of being good. And he had no intention of staying inside the potting shed. So, with a foul-smelling burp-filled growl, he once again cocked one leg in the air and then he huffed… and he puffed… and with the power of a force-ten hurricane HE FARTED THE SHED DOWN!!

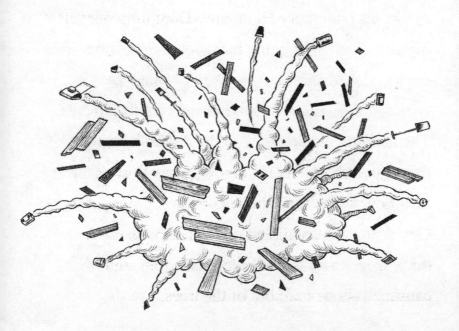

Chapter six

For minutes after the massive eruption tremors rippled through the town and beyond.

In his laboratory Humphrey Dumpling dusted himself down after being thrown headlong across the room. Gingerly, he crunched towards the window over broken glass and ruined experiments. The garden was strewn with the debris from the devastated shed. The lawnmower was floating in next door's pond and their statuette set of Seaburn City's first eleven all had new plant-pot hats. A thick green vapour filled the air, its foul stink causing owls to faint out of the trees.

There was, however, no sign of the Were-Bob. Suddenly, the silence was shattered by an almighty clatter. It had come from the kitchen. Humphrey crept warily along the hallway and peeked through the door. There, kneeling on the tiled floor, was the Were-Bob demolishing with giant bites the side of beef that had been roasting in the oven. Humphrey couldn't help but gasp. In a flash the Were-Bob swivelled around 180° and his steely stare locked onto Humphrey. Then he roared the roar of a thousand lions, which knocked his host clean off his feet once again. Humphrey scrambled back up then scuttled down to the cellar where he could lock himself in good and proper.

Humphrey's appearance had been but a minor distraction to the Were-Bob. Now, his only focus

was on his desperate hunt for food. His rumbling
tummy seemed to be drumming out his desire
to EAT, EAT, EAT. And what he wanted to EAT,
EAT, EAT was MEAT, MEAT, MEAT – the fuel
of the werewolf. But unless it was a full Moon,
Humphrey was a devoted vegetarian. So, with the
side of beef all gobbled up, there wasn't so much
as a mini-chipolata left anywhere in the kitchen.

The Were-Bob crashed out into the dark
night. As if on automatic
pilot, he tore up Puddle
Lane, his sensitive
nose picking up the
carnivorous smells
wafting from the premier
meaty restaurant in town,
the HOUSE OF BONES.
Nothing and
nobody could
stop him.

Here, there and everywhere, terrified townsfolk jumped into hedges, cowered behind walls and shook in phone boxes.

At the HOUSE OF BONES the Were-Bob, not much caring for doors, smashed through the restaurant's front window. Panic broke out. Faint-hearted diners clambered over each other to escape, leaving half-eaten steaks and hot dogs. Without a second thought, the Were-Bob wolfed them all down. Still, though, his appetite wasn't satisfied. His beady eyes settled on a 'BIG MEATY BUCKET BIN.' In seconds he polished off twelve whammy burgers, eleven lamb kebabs, ten T-bone steaks, nine chicken nuggets, eight sausage hot-pots, seven turkey drummers, six chilli hot dogs, five onion rings, four scotch eggs, three pork pies, two ham joints and a partridge-not-in-a-pear-tree.

Having licked the bucket dry and gulped a final mini pork pie for luck, his stomach was finally full of fuel. His soul, on the other hand,

was full of trouble. What followed was a night of mayhem. In no time at all, the town was in disarray. Sirens everywhere were whooping and whirring. Trees were uprooted. Bins were alight. Windows were smashed. Flowerbeds were destroyed. The hoots of horns were competing with each other as cars queued to get out of the town. And above, as the clouds rolled in again, the birds were leaving too, flying off into the dark, nervous night.

Through all of this, not one person realised that Bob and the Were-Bob were one and the

same being. Gone was all trace of the model
citizen who helped cats stuck in trees and got
miffed about un-poopy-scooped streets and ripped
denim jeans.

But there was one thing that the Were-Bob
had in common with the real Bob – a sudden,
overwhelming desire TO GET TO THE MOON!!

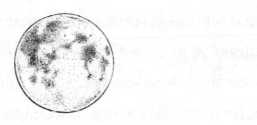

Chapter seven

Having been the target of the Were-Bob's stone-throwing, the hands of the town clock had stopped at 8.53 precisely. Had they still been ticking they would have revealed that there was less than an hour until midnight. Somehow though, the Were-Bob knew that midnight was drawing near, and that this was important.

His boundless energy was showing no sign of slowing down but, with the town already in ruins, the Were-Bob was running out of mischief to make. In the middle of throwing a mud pie at the last remaining billboard, suddenly he stopped dead in his tracks. His attention had been caught by his latest billboard target:

Suddenly, a spark ignited inside the Were-Bob as he stared at the huge picture. There was something familiar about the fresh-faced spaceman with his terribly smart hairstyle and smiley expression. Of course, terribly smart hairstyles and smiley expressions are two of the nicey-nicey things that werewolves instinctively hate. A red-raw rage soared up inside the Were-Bob and with all the force he could muster, he slung his mud pie slap bang into the poster boy's face.

Still though, the larger part of the advert, depicting a huge full Moon, held the Were-Bob's gaze. He felt a strange pull towards it. And that strange pull became a thousand times stronger when, high above him, the clouds parted once more. Now the Moon on the poster was more than matched by the real thing shining through the darkness. It was then he knew. For some reason he had to get to the real Moon before midnight. It was his destiny.

At once, the Were-Bob's instincts kicked in. Though by nature werewolves are not experienced astronauts, without even knowing it, the Were-Bob was able to draw on the vast knowledge buried deep inside Bob. A glint on the horizon caught the Were-Bob's eye. It was moonlight reflecting off Bob's rocket at the Lunar Hill launch-pad. With his inner clock telling him not to hang about, the

Were-Bob was off. Spotting an abandoned 21A bus, he pounced behind the wheel and erratically sped away. All the passengers had long since fled, apart from little Granny Lavender, who was rather vexed about the change of driver mid-route. If she was late for the wrestling she would have a stiff letter of complaint to write to the bus company.

"YOUNG MAN!" shouted little Granny Lavender. "THE WRESTLING ARENA IS THE OTHER WAY! I'M GOING TO MISS BIG DADDY HAYSTACKS AGAINST Y-FRONTS McSOCKEM!"

The wrestling arena, however was not along the new route on which the Were-Bob was taking the 21A bus. He could see Bob's rocket and, ignoring all the roads, he took the straightest line

possible towards it. The bus ploughed through hedges, fields and gardens, narrowly avoiding cows, ponds and sheds.

Granny Lavender's complaints were drowned out by the whirring sirens of a hundred and one cars that were suddenly in hot pursuit and gaining on the bus. Each had blacked-out windows and the letters D.O.N.U.T. written in silver on the side. It was the DEFENDERS OF THE NOBLE UNIVERSE TASKFORCE – the toughest police force in the galaxy.

Up above, D.O.N.U.T. helicopters joined the dramatic chase; it was obvious they considered the Were-Bob a major danger. As the 21A bus bumped to the launch-pad, the Were-Bob's sensitive ears recognised one voice in particular within the chasing pack and understood.

"FOR GOODNESS' SAKE LADS!" cried Humphrey Dumpling over his radio. "WE CAN'T LET HIM GET TO THE MOON! AT MIDNIGHT HE'LL INVOKE THE CURSE OF THE WEREFLEAS!"

Chapter eight

By the time the D.O.N.U.T. agents arrived at
Lunar Hill, they had seen the 21A bus career
around the other side and then heard it screech to
a halt. One by one the D.O.N.U.T. cars pulled up,
forming an arc behind which the agents crouched,
each with a tranquiliser gun at the ready. After
a few tense minutes, they sensed movement.
Humphrey Dumpling braced himself for a
whirlwind of trouble.

"HE'S COMING LADS!" he warned. "BE
PREPARED – HE'S A MEANY BEAST!"

Just then a silhouetted figure emerged from around the hill. As expected it was a growling, grumbling ball of fury, intent only on mischief. Special agent Barnaby Teapot-Smythe, Director of D.O.N.U.T., wasted no time. "FIRE, FIRE, FIRE!!!" he ordered, and fire the agents did. A volley of tranquiliser darts zipped through the darkness before successfully hitting their target who doddered, staggered and then slumped to the ground with a thud.

Immediately Humphrey and the D.O.N.U.T. agents moved in, just as the target muttered a few slurred words.

"Blooming… bus companies… changing routes willy-nilly without a… thought… for us… poor pensioners. Well… stiff letter…. coming

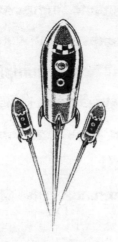

their way… I can…. tell you!"

Barnaby Teapot-Smythe was a little
surprised. "Well," he said, "I was expecting this
Were-Bob chappy to look a bit more fierce than
that, I must say!"

But Humphrey Dumpling was aghast.
"THAT'S NOT HIM!" he said. "THAT'S AN OLD
LADY! WE'VE GOT THE WRONG PERSON!"

Indeed, lying asleep in front of them with a
bottom full of darts was little Granny Lavender.
Nobody knew where the Were-Bob was, until a
great rumbling boom broke out above their heads.

Everything shook as dark plumes of smoke danced around white-hot flames.

"THE ROCKET!" cried Humphrey. "IT'S TAKING OFF!" He was right. Up and up and up it zoomed, with a furry and determined face visible through the porthole.

As the rocket approached the Moon, things looked different. Gone was the warm, friendly atmosphere. In its place was a cold, unfamiliar eeriness. The real Bob would have been totally heartbroken but he was locked away somewhere deep, deep down inside the Were-Bob and he wouldn't be back until after the full Moon had passed. By then, it would be too late.

The rocket landed with less than a minute to go until midnight. The moment had almost come and even the Were-Bob wasn't quite sure what was going to happen. From Earth he could hear the D.O.N.U.T. rockets blasting upwards in hot pursuit. But they would never make it in time.

The Were-Bob set foot on the Moon like the king of a conquering army. His wereflea bites had also made him tolerant to the cosmic conditions, so he didn't need a suit or a helmet. He could hear the D.O.N.U.T. rockets getting closer and Humphrey Dumpling shouting over a loudspeaker.

"BOB!" pleaded Humphrey. "I KNOW YOU'RE IN THAT BEAST SOMEWHERE. THE EARTH, THE MOON AND THE STARS ARE IN DANGER. PLEASE HELP US!"

But it seemed his words were in vain. The Were-Bob stood, chest out and eyes steely. His inner clock was counting down. There were 5 seconds to go until crunch time, then 4 and 3 and 2 and 1. The moment had come; it was midnight on the night of the full Moon and the Were-Bob began to HOWL! He began to howl and he didn't stop. It was frightening. It was deafening! The universe shook. Stars flickered and comets turned around and flew the other way. Then, something strange began to happen. THE SURFACE OF THE MOON BEGAN TO CHANGE! IT WAS BECOMING DARK AND PRICKLY! LIKE A COWBOY'S CHIN... IT WAS GROWING STUBBLE!

Chapter nine

Bob and the Moon had always been like two peas in a pod. Both were wholesome and clean-cut. Now, tragically, what had happened to Bob earlier that evening was being mirrored on the Moon.

As the Were-Bob howled, the stubble grew and grew, covering the entire lunar landscape like a neatly kept lawn. Rapidly, it lengthened to resemble a terribly neglected lawn, un-mowed for weeks. But of course, it wasn't grass that was growing. It was hair… and it was dangerous.

This was the true curse of the werefleas. At a pace, the hair crept upwards, first swishing over the Were-Bob's ankles, then up over his knees, waist and chest. Soon he was swallowed up by a vast, fuzzy jungle.

Down below, the D.O.N.U.T. rockets had opened their emergency battle hatches and special combat scissors had emerged alongside catapults loaded with bombs of hair-removal cream. Like giant Swiss Army knives they fearlessly advanced on the fuzzball Were-Moon.

The fuzzball Were-Moon was ready though. Now, long, untamed pigtail-like strands shot up from all points out into space and thrashed around like the arms of a ticked-off octopus. One by one the D.O.N.U.T. rockets were swatted back towards Earth. They stood no chance.

"WE'RE NOT BLOOMIN' HAIRDRESSERS!" Barnaby Teapot-Smythe bellowed to Humphrey Dumpling. With a heavy heart, he ordered a full retreat. Ominously, the ever-growing pigtails followed, prodding the rockets all the way, before creeping down through Earth's clouds and snaking around the mountains and skyscrapers and other tall stuff.

On the Were-Moon the cries of panic from the people of Earth went in one of the Were-Bob's long, pointy ears and out the other. He didn't care that Earth would soon become a matted and tattered ball of hair. He didn't care that the pigtails were beginning to slither their way towards Mars and Jupiter and all the other planets. And he didn't care that the sun itself would be finally swamped, leading to the death of the solar system and everything in it.

The curse of the werefleas had proven far stronger than Humphrey Dumpling could have ever imagined. Why would two simple fleas want to create such mayhem? Humphrey's vast knowledge of fleas, gained through years of mind-boggling experiments and brain-draining research had led him to the only conclusion scientifically possible – that Hubert and Margot had just been very, VERY naughty fleas.

Having been booted back to Earth by those pesky pigtails, Humphrey now sat on the eighteenth floor of Infinity House, the Earth's headquarters of the big entire universe. He was in the office of Tarantula Van Trumpet, Head of the Department for Moon Affairs and outside the attacking pigtails were running rampant amidst wild flurries of snow-like flakes that gracefully drifted down and settled, giving the world an oddly festive feel.

"Dandruff," remarked Humphrey to Tarantula and closed the window.

Humphrey was anxiously pacing the floor. "We can't beat this with cutting and snipping," he said. "We have to stop it at the source: the Were-Bob. Stop his howling and I think the curse will be broken."

"But we can't get near him," argued Tarantula.

"True," replied Humphrey "We can't but perhaps he can!" Humphrey was pointing at a clean-cut face on the wall of Astro-portraits. It was BOB! "But how on Earth can we reawaken our Bob to fight the Were-Bob from the inside?"

Coolly, Tarantula took off his glasses, cleaned them with his hankie and then put them back on.

"I might know a way," he said.

Chapter ten

Back up in space the Were-Moon was now just a small part of the big, bad, grizzly fuzzball that was the solar system. Planets, moons, comets and stars were all interwoven into the gigantic mesh of a million, billion, trillion strands of hair. The rapidly advancing pigtails were about to launch their attack on the sun. In minutes, they would snuff out its light and that would be the end of everything.

Meanwhile, on the Moon, the Were-Bob continued his robotic howling without a break. The anxious voices from Earth were still reaching his super-sharp ears, but nothing and nobody pricked his conscience – because he didn't have

one. All hope was lost.

Then, as if by magic, something AMAZING happened. Through the never-ending babble one lone, quiet voice found a tiny chink in the Were-Bob's armour.

"Bob!" it said. "We need you, come back to us." It was as if a bolt of lightning had hit the Were-Bob. For just a few seconds the howling stopped. The Were-Bob was confused. For that flicker of a moment he had felt different – kinder and more pleasant. Then the curse took over and he howled again. But not for long. The mysterious voice spoke once more.

"Bob, I know that somewhere in there you can hear me. PLEASE come back!"

The Were-Bob stopped howling for a second time. Again he was bamboozled. Now, looking around the Moon, he was getting sudden urges to vacuum, dust and polish.

For a third time he attempted to howl but it

was becoming more difficult. His howls were weaker and less powerful. Good was beginning to course through his veins! And he couldn't stop it! The curse wasn't as strong as the mysterious voice. It was calling to Bob and somewhere deep,

deep down inside the Were-Bob, the Man on the Moon was responding.

Against his will, the Were-Bob was feeling soothed. And, as his howling weakened, so did the grip of the werefleas' curse. The violent thrashing of the Moon's pigtails had quietened to a gentle swishing. The blizzards of dandruff were clearing and, most importantly, the attack on the sun was halted.

There was a battle taking place inside the Were-Bob. Despite his desperate need to howl, he just couldn't. He was too concerned with staring at his shoeless feet and worrying about what the other astronauts would think. The mysterious voice was pulling Bob back. For the second time that evening a transformation was taking place.

Getting louder all the time, it was as if the voice was drawing closer.

"HOLD ON BOB!" it said, "I'M NEARLY WITH YOU. STAY STRONG!"

Bob was strong and he was getting stronger. His personality was beginning to dominate the Were-Bob more and more. Thoughts of bingo, crosswords and chocolate-covered nuts returned ten-fold. He wondered about the football results and whether the fancy teapot shop would open on Bank Holiday Monday. The Were-Bob was almost Bob again.

But only almost. One last time the remainder of the Were-Bob's dastardly character summoned up whatever energy he had left. Like a spluttering engine he took a deep, deep breath

and attempted to howl again.

"H... H... HOWWW..." he tried.
"H H... HOOW... HOOWWW...
HOOWWWLLOVELY IT WOULD BE TO
HAVE A NICE CUP OF TEA!!!"

With those words, the universe clicked back into place. It was official. BOB WAS BACK! And extremely confused.

"I'M A HIPPY!!" he cried, looking down at his long beard.

"Don't worry," said the mysterious voice, which was very close now. "I'll explain everything in a few seconds."

Bob watched wide-eyed as, right in front of him, the swishing forest of hair parted and a small, brown-and-white, six-legged creature emerged. It was a dog!

"BARRY!!" cheered Bob.

"BOB!!" cheered Barry.

At last Bob and his best-ever friend,

Barry, were together again. They hugged each other tightly. And that's when Bob realised… IT WAS BARRY THAT WAS THE MYSTERIOUS VOICE! BUT HOW COULD BOB UNDERSTAND HIS WOOFS?

"Don't worry," Barry woofed. "You've been a werewolf. Werewolf and dog language is very similar."

Then another voice sounded through the hair.

"It'll wear off in a jiffy!" shouted the voice and then Humphrey Dumpling appeared. He was carrying Bob's, suit, boots and helmet. "You'd better put these on," he said. "Your body will be back to normal any time now. Here's some soap and a razor – you'll want to look spick and span for your hero's welcome."

"But I didn't do anything," said Bob.

"Yes you did," replied Humphrey. "You broke the curse of the werefleas and saved the entire solar system."

"But how?" asked Bob.

Humphrey put his hand on the spaceman's shoulder. "By being yourself, Bob," he told him. "Good old Tarantula knew that the love between you and Barry was probably the only thing strong enough to get through the Were-Bob's defences. Barnaby Teapot-Smythe acted immediately and every D.O.N.U.T agent on Earth was tasked with finding your best-ever friend. In the end it was special agent Tarquin

Fromage who found him, asleep in a cardboard box under the flyover above the robot factory. It seems the Flea-Buster 3000 you gave him had protected Barry from the werefleas, but not from the Were-Bob you turned into while you were sleepwalking. Barry had no idea what was happening to you, so when the Were-Bob threw him out, he thought it was you doing it. He was homeless and heartbroken. When Tarquin called, I rushed to the scene, armed with a bowl of bone soup and my doggy phrase book. The rest is history."

And so too was the hairy Moon and the fuzzball it had sprouted. All that remained was for the D.O.N.U.T. agents to spend a few months firing hair-removal cream bombs across the solar system. Then they would shave, snip and clip the whole thing back to normal.

Bob dusted off his old lawnmower from the shed and, with his best-ever friend, Barry, got to

work on setting the Moon to rights. It had been a close shave, but the Moon was soon, once again, bald and beautiful – just the way Bob, Barry and the space tourists liked it.

WA[NTED]

FOR HAIRY
AGAINST

HUBERT
THE TERRIBLY
NAUGHTY FLEA

REWARD

(and one free
mini-scotch egg)

THE END